COLOR THE VOTE

Written by Elsie Guerrero
Cover Designed by Jasmine Mills | Illustrated by Tullip Studio

ISBN -13: 979-8-3304-3417-6

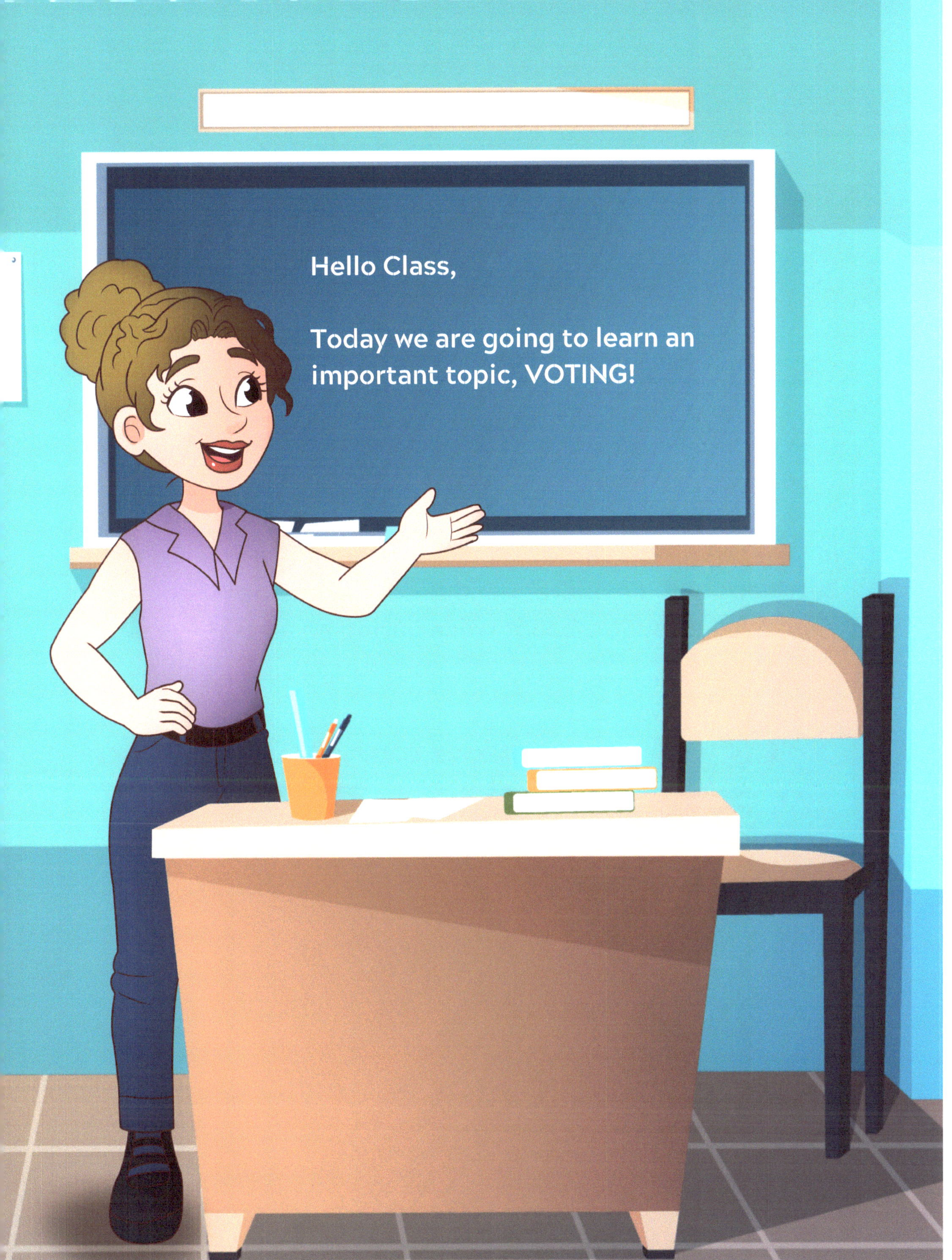
Hello Class,
Today we are going to learn an important topic, VOTING!

In the United States, voting is a formal indication of a choice between two or more candidates or courses of action expressed through a ballot twice during an election year.

There are three types of elections where we can vote: General, Midterm, and Special election.

In the general election, we vote for a president, federal, state, and local representatives. In the midterm election, we vote for state governor, federal, state, and local representatives. Special Elections are rare and only occur when there is a vacant position.

We have representation in all three levels of government: federal, state, and local, which gives us many opportunities to vote.

Federal

State

Local

Voting gives people a voice. Voting is important because it gives the people the power to elect who they want to be represent them.

In the general election, we vote for the president and vice president to enforce the laws of the United States.

Every two years, we elect the U.S. House of Representatives to work in Congress to create laws. They will always be part of the general and midterm election.

The U.S. Senators will also be part of the midterm and general elections. However, not all of the Senators run at the same time. Approximately one-third of the Senators run every election.

At the state level, we vote for a governor and state representatives. Every state in the United States has a governor and representative in their district. We also vote for the State Attorney General, who represents the state and state agencies before the state and federal courts. These candidates can be on the ballots for either the general or midterm elections.

At the local level, we vote for a mayor and city councils. We also vote for our district attorney, who is in charge of representing the government in criminal cases and is responsible for ensuring that justice is served by prosecuting individuals accused of committing crimes. These candidates can also be on the ballots for either the general or midterm elections.

We have so many opportunities to vote. We vote every two years at every level of the government: local, state, and federal.

The right to vote was not always given. In the past, some people did not have the right to vote, such as African Americans and women. But thanks to the government updating the constitution, they have the right to vote.

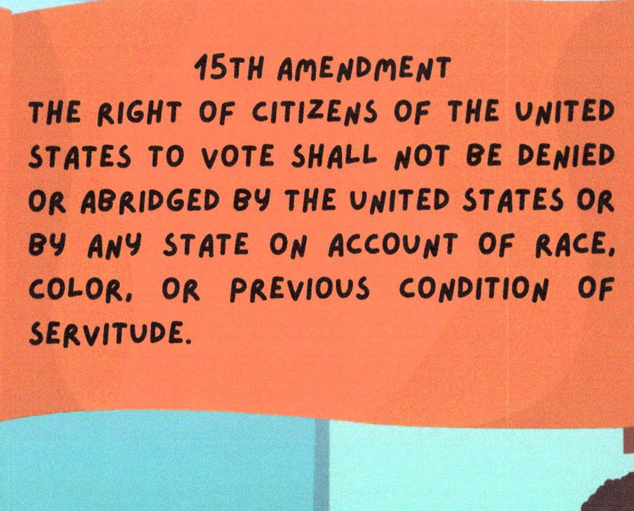

The 15th Amendment gave African Americans the right to vote.

The 19th Amendment gave women the right to vote.
19TH AMENDMENT
THE RIGHT OF CITIZENS OF THE UNITED STATES TO VOTE SHALL NOT BE DENIED OR ABRIDGED BY THE UNITED STATES OR BY ANY STATE ON ACCOUNT OF SEX.

The 26th Amendment established a minimum age requirement to vote. Anyone over the age of 18 can vote. However, some states and local governments allow people who are 16 or 17 to vote.

26TH AMENDMENT

THE RIGHT OF CITIZENS OF THE UNITED STATES, WHO ARE EIGHTEEN YEARS OF AGE OR OLDER, TO VOTE SHALL NOT BE DENIED OR ABRIDGED BY THE UNITED STATES OR BY ANY STATE ON ACCOUNT OF AGE.

Although everyone over the age of 18 has the right to vote in the United States, often time we come across big problems in certain states. Not everyone has access to their right to vote.

Voter suppression is an approach used to influence the outcome of an election by preventing specific groups of people from voting.

Sometimes, polling places will not let people vote if they do not have a photo ID.

Other times, polling places will not let people vote if their name does not match the name on the ID. Usually, it is people with two last names or who were recently married.

Although there are people in the United States who are legal residents, polling places do not let people vote if they are not US citizens. However, there are places where legal residents can vote in local elections.

Other times, people move to a new location and not often updated with the secretary of state office, causing polling places to not let them vote on election day.

Purge is a system that is needed to update the voting registration system. It normally removes outdated information. However, there are instances where people who are eligible to vote are taken off the list with little to no awareness, causing many people to be unable to vote on the day of the election.

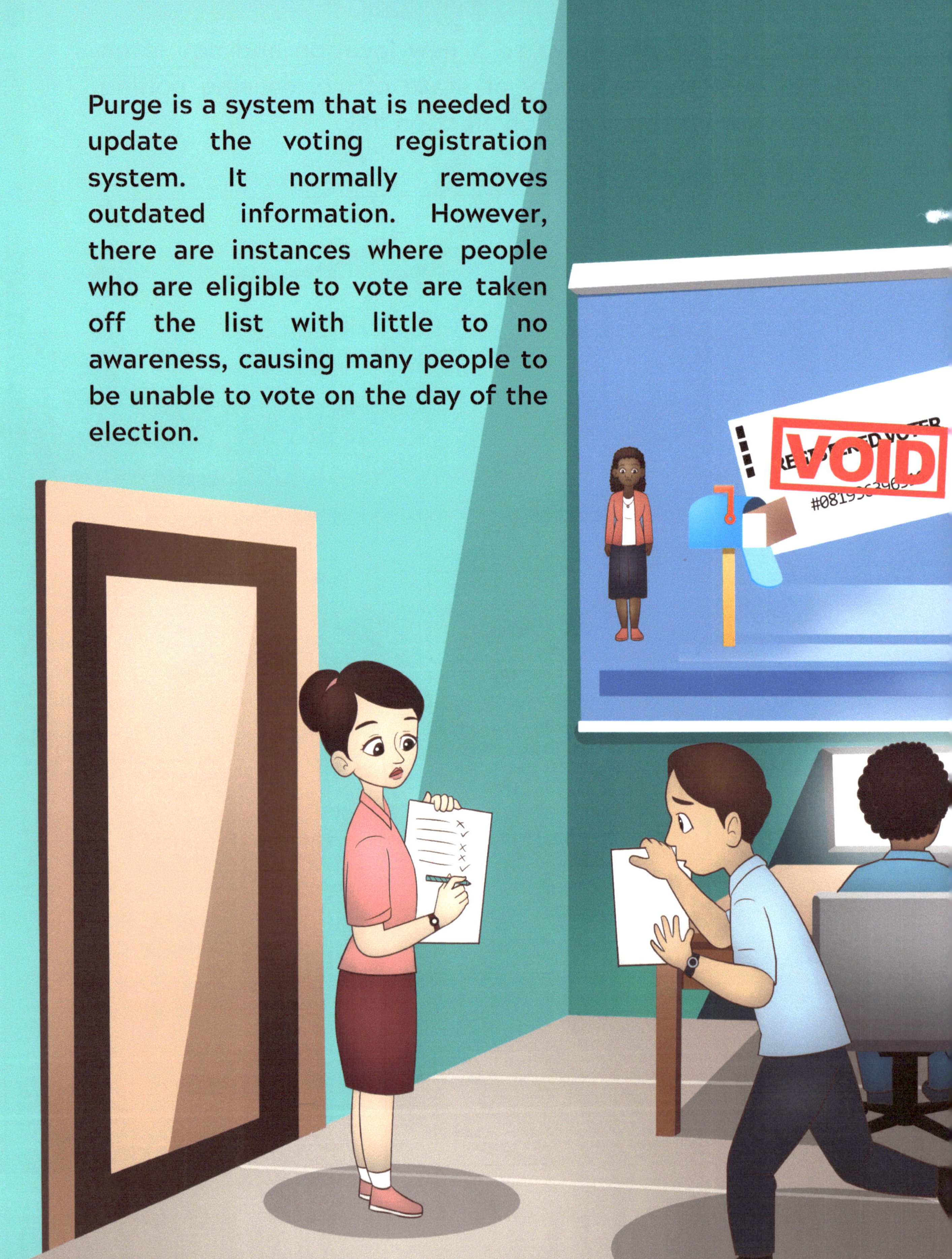

Voting is very important and it is a fundamental right. Everyone who is at least 18 years old and, in some cases, does not have a criminal record, has the right to vote.

We need to exercise our right to vote. The people we elect are the people who make the decisions that impact us the most!

After learning why it is important to vote, you can act in three big ways.

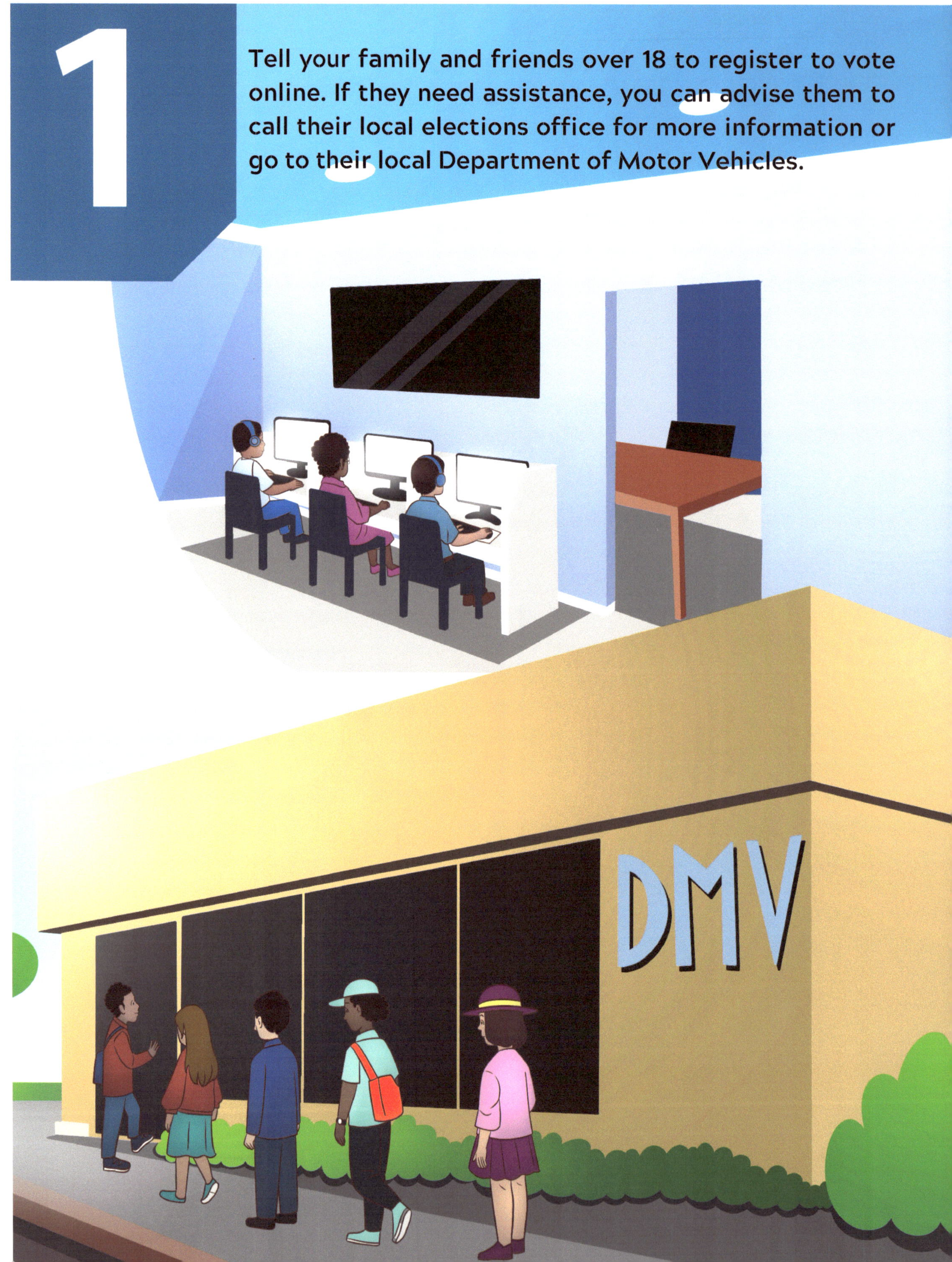
1
Tell your family and friends over 18 to register to vote online. If they need assistance, you can advise them to call their local elections office for more information or go to their local Department of Motor Vehicles.
DMV

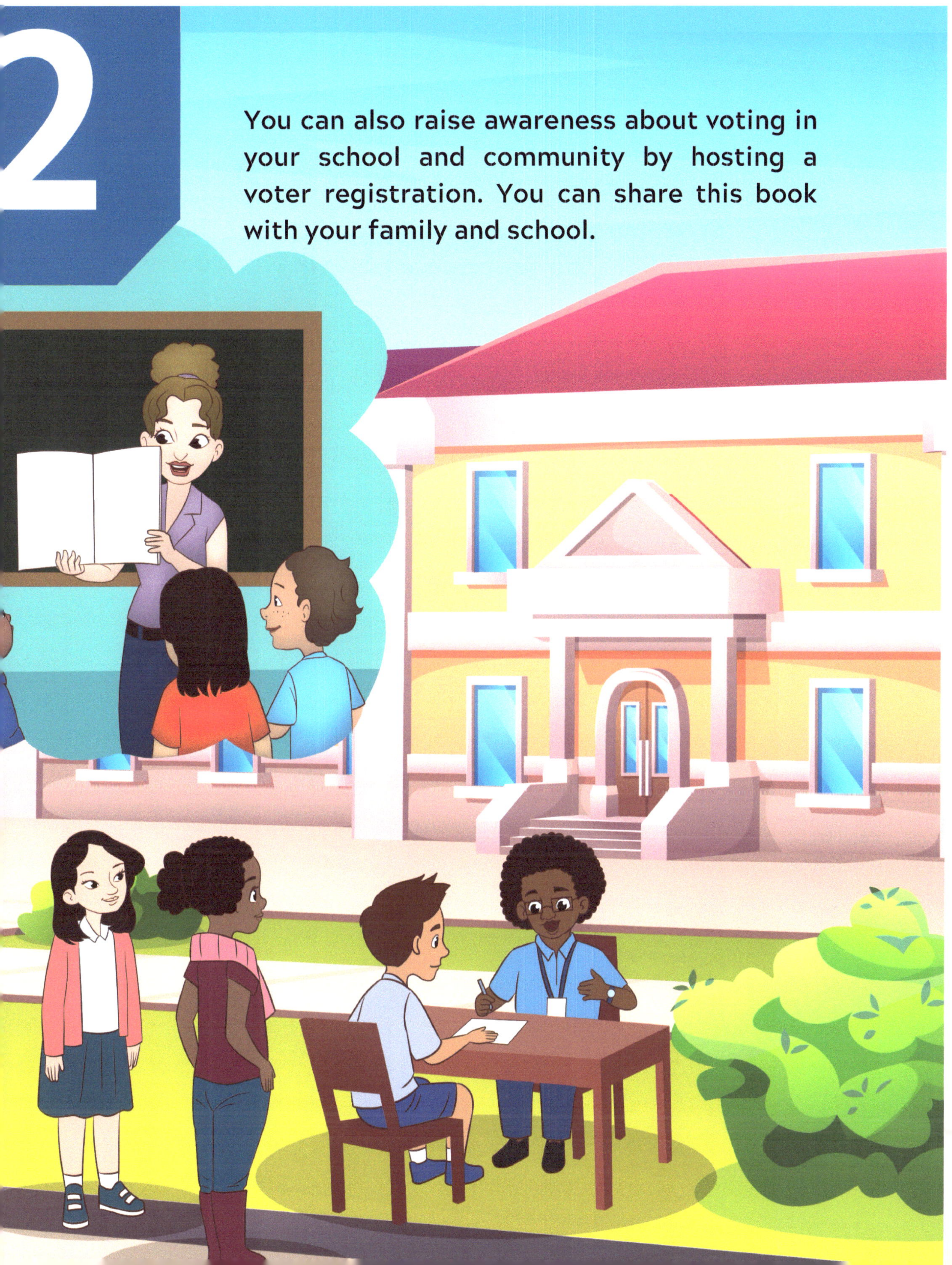

2

You can also raise awareness about voting in your school and community by hosting a voter registration. You can share this book with your family and school.

3

You can create a mock election at school and highlight the importance of voting.

Can you think of other ways to raise awareness about the importance of voting? You have the power to make effective change. Make sure everyone you know register to vote and vote on election day.

Vote! Your life depends on this!

For more information on voting registration, please visit your state secretary office or visit www.usa.gov/voting

Glossary

Ballot: a process of voting in writing and typically in secret.

Congress: a national legislative body, especially that of the US. The US Congress, which meets at the Capitol in Washington, D.C., was established by the Constitution of 1787 and is composed of the Senate and the House of Representatives.

District: an area of a country or city, especially one regarded as a distinct unit because of a particular characteristic.

District Attorney: a public official who acts as a prosecutor for the state or the federal government in court in a particular district.

Federal Government: Consists of the White House, Congress, and federal courts and agencies.

General Election: a regular election for statewide or national offices.

Legal resident: A person who is not a citizen of the United States, but is legally able to live in the United States.

Local Government: the administration of a particular town, county, or district, with representatives elected by those who live there.

Mock election: an election held to call for free and fair elections, whether for educational demonstration, amusement, or political protest.

Purges: the system of cleaning up voter rolls by deleting names from registration lists.

State Attorney: This person serves as a counselor to state government agencies and legislatures and as a representative of the public interest.

State Government: Consists of the governor, state legislatures, and state courts and agencies.

Follow, like, and subscribe to Promote Inclusion Books

@promoteinclusionbooks

@promoteinclusionbooks

Promote Inclusion Books

Promote Inclusion Books

@inclusionbooks

Check out other books written by Elsie Guerrero

SPREAD AWARENESS. PROMOTE INCLUSION

www.promoteinclusion.com

www.ingramcontent.com/pod-product-compliance
Ingram Content Group UK Ltd.
Pitfield, Milton Keynes, MK11 3LW, UK
UKHW060117300726
14090UKWH00002B/238

9798330434176